# The Pumpkin Fair

by Eve Bunting / Illustrated by Eileen Christelow

CLARION BOOKS/New York

Clarion Books
a Houghton Mifflin Company imprint
215 Park Avenue South, New York, NY 10003
Text copyright © 1997 by Eve Bunting
Illustrations copyright © 1997 by Eileen Christelow

The illustrations for this book were executed in pen, ink, and watercolor on Lanaquarelle.
The text was set in 16/22-point Italia.

For information about permission to reproduce selections from this book, write to Permissions,
Houghton Mifflin Company, 215 Park Avenue South, New York, NY 10003.

For information about this and other Houghton Mifflin trade and reference books and multimedia
products, visit The Bookstore at Houghton Mifflin on the World Wide Web at (http://www.hmco.com/trade/).

Printed in Singapore

**Library of Congress Cataloging-in-Publication Data**

Bunting, Eve, 1928–
    Pumpkin fair / by Eve Bunting ; illustrated by Eileen Christelow.
        p.    cm.
Summary: A rather ordinary pumpkin wins a prize for "the best-loved pumpkin at the fair,
the best-loved pumpkin anywhere."
ISBN 0-395-70060-4
    [1. Pumpkin—Fiction.    2. Fairs—Fiction.    3. Stories in rhyme.]  I. Christelow, Eileen, ill.  II. Title.
PZ8.3.B92Pu    1997
[E]—dc20    96-20626
CIP
AC

TWP  10  9  8  7  6  5  4  3  2

For Peter, Peter,
Pumpkin Eater
with love
—E. B.

I'm going to the Pumpkin Fair.
Pumpkins, pumpkins everywhere!
"These ones here were grown from seed—
Yes sir, yes sir, yes indeed!
The biggest pumpkin ever seen,
the smallest one there's ever been!"

Mine's in between, hand grown by me.
(I got the pumpkin seed for free.)
It has a lot of shiny dots.
I call them pumpkin beauty spots.

The boy next door thinks he's so smart—
He says each one's a pumpkin wart.
I cover up my pumpkin's ears—
She'll feel so awful if she hears!

Mister Pumpkin shakes my hand.
And there's the Peter Pumpkin Band.

The Pumpkin Princess has a crown
Of little pumpkins, all glued down.

12

"Pumpkin bowling! Roll a few!"
(Pumpkin dear, I won't roll you!)

"Toss the pumpkin through the net!"
Oops! A pumpkin omelette.

"Tug o' war! Just hold on tight—
Tug and tug with all your might."
Slipping . . . slipping . . . sliding . . . *splash*!
We're in a bed of pumpkin mash.

Juggle pumpkins, one two three.
"If you touch mine, you're *history!*"

I like spitting pumpkin seeds.
They're smooth and white, like little beads.

"Pucker up and let 'em fly!
Spit 'em far and spit 'em high!"

Pumpkin creatures in a row.
"How are you? Hello! Hello!"
Mouse and pig and kitty cat,
Rabbit, snake, and vampire bat.

23

There's pumpkin cake and pumpkin pie.
Eat until you think you'll die.
Pumpkin ice cream, cookies too.

There's even gooey party stew.
(I'll try them all, except the stew.
It's icky-looking, gross, pee-yew!)

It's time for prizes, time for fame.
I know they'll never call my name.
My pumpkin isn't very big.
She's not a mouse or dog or pig.
I tell her that it's still OK.
She's very special in her way.

And then . . . and then . . . how can it be?
The Pumpkin Master's calling me!

"The best-loved pumpkin at the fair.
The best-loved pumpkin anywhere!"
I get a ribbon, red and blue.
My pumpkin gets a ribbon, too.
How did they know? How did they see
The way I felt inside of me?

It's growing dark, but through the night
The jack-o'-lanterns shine so bright.
We all hold hands and sing a song
Of pumpkins round and pumpkins long,
Of pumpkins fat and pumpkins lean
And pumpkins somewhere in between.

"Good night! Good night! Sleep tight! Take care!
See you at next year's Pumpkin Fair!"